A Day at the Fair

Arleta Richardson

Illustrated by Mary O'Keefe Young

Chariot Books™

*A Division of Cook
Communications Ministries*

Chariot Books™ is an imprint of Chariot Family Publishing
Cook Communications Ministries, Elgin, Illinois 60120
Cook Communications Ministries, Paris, Ontario
Kingsway Communications, Eastbourne, England

A DAY AT THE FAIR
© 1995 by Arleta Richardson for text and Mary O'Keefe Young for illustrations

Book design by Paetzold Design
First printing, 1995
Printed in the United States of America
99 98 97 96 95   5 4 3 2 1
ISBN 0-7814-0249-2

Originally published as "When Grandma Needed Prayer" in *More Stories from Grandma's Attic*, by Arleta Richardson. © 1979 David C. Cook Publishing Company.
Adapted for this edition by Catherine L. Davis

I will never forget the stories my grandmother told me about growing up on the family farm in Michigan. Grandma had a story for every occasion. This is one she told me when I'd lost a library book. After Grandma and I prayed that the Lord would help me find it, I found it under my pillow when I went to get ready for bed.

"Grandma," I said, "we didn't really have to pray. The book was here anyway, and the Lord knew I needed it."

"Get into bed," Grandma said, "and I'll tell you why we should always pray, even though God knows our needs . . ."

When I was about six years old, my Pa promised that the whole family could go with him to the country fair in the next county. He wanted to attend the cattle auction. "I hear there is a cooking and sewing exhibit for the ladies,"

he said to Ma. "You will enjoy that."

I was so excited I could hardly wait for the day to come.

The day of the fair we were up before daybreak to have breakfast and get started. I was in such a hurry to leave that I didn't want to finish the meal. But Ma said I'd better eat all of it.

After breakfast, Pa reached for the Bible.

"Oh, Pa!" I protested. "We aren't going to take time for prayer this morning, are we?"

Pa looked at me with surprise. "God always comes first in this house, Mabel. We want to start our day by talking to Him."

"Well, *I* don't," I replied crossly.

Ma didn't punish me for my sassy answer. She just looked at me and said quietly, "All right, Mabel, you won't need to pray this morning."

As we started out, somehow the day didn't seem quite as exciting to me. I knew I had behaved badly. But as we neared the fairgrounds, I began to think of the fun I would have.

"The first thing I want to do is find Sarah Jane."

"You won't have far to look," Ma replied. "I see her standing by the buggies, waiting for you."

Sarah Jane was hopping from one foot to the other with excitement. "Hurry, Mabel," she called. "I've been waiting and waiting for you. What took you so long?"

I started to say we just *had* to pray before we could leave, but thought better of it. "We're here now," I said. "Let's go."

We ran off toward the big tent that held the cooking and sewing exhibit, and our mothers followed close behind.

"Oh," Sarah Jane exclaimed, "we'll never see all this! I didn't know there were that many quilts in the whole world! Have you ever seen so many things?"

For a long time Sarah Jane and I walked along with our mothers, looking at the displays and pointing out what we liked best.

Shortly before noon, the ladies sat down to rest.

"May we go outside and look around, Ma?"
I asked.

"I guess that would be all right. But don't get out of sight of the tents, will you?"

"Oh, no," we promised. "We'll stay right close by."

Near the edge of the grounds Sarah Jane stopped and grabbed my hand. "Look, Mabel. Do you see that?" She pointed toward the big trees.

"What is it? Maybe a calf from the animal tent?"

Sarah Jane shook her head. "I don't think so.
It looks like a fawn to me. Let's go see."

Quietly, we tiptoed toward the trees. It was a
fawn, and it was watching us.

"He doesn't seem to be afraid," I said.

As we came closer, the fawn turned and started into the woods. But he walked slowly and let us keep him in sight.

"Isn't he pretty?" Sarah Jane exclaimed. "I wish he'd stop and let us pet him."

We followed the fawn for a long time. Finally he disappeared from sight and we decided we'd better get back.

"We've come a long way," I said. "I can't see the edge of the woods from here. What if we go in the wrong direction?"

"You can't go in the wrong direction if you just turn around from the way you've been going," Sarah Jane said. And to prove it, she turned around and started back. I followed.

We walked on for what seemed like a long time; then Sarah Jane stopped.

"We don't seem to be going anyplace," she said. "I don't think we walked this far."

"You mean you don't know the way back? You acted like you did."

"I guess we didn't turn around far enough," Sarah Jane admitted. "We'd better stop and think about it a minute."

The woods didn't seem as friendly anymore.

"Sarah Jane," I said, "I'm getting sort of worried. Besides, I'm awfully hungry. Do you suppose they'll go ahead and eat without us?"

"Probably," Sarah Jane replied glumly. "They won't know we went away from the grounds. We were sure dumb to follow that fawn."

We stood for a few minutes, staring into the woods. Then Sarah Jane said, "I think we'd better pray about it. The Lord can help us find the way back."

Suddenly I remembered that I had refused to pray that morning. Now I was sorry and ashamed to ask God for help.

"You pray," I said to Sarah Jane as we sat down.

"Dear Lord, please send someone to find us," she prayed. "Thank You."

"Now what shall we do?" she asked.

"Pa told us that if we ever got lost in our woods we should sit still until someone finds us. Maybe we better do that in this woods, too."

"I guess so. We didn't do much good moving around, so we'd better stay right here."

It seemed like we sat on that log for hours. We sang all the songs we knew, and recited all the poems we had learned.

"Do you suppose we had better remind God that we're still here?" Sarah Jane asked.

"I don't think we need to. I'm sure He's already told our folks where we are."

"I wish they would hurry up and come then," Sarah Jane said. "It must be almost night."

Finally both of us fell asleep.

The next thing we knew we were being picked up in strong arms and carried toward the fairgrounds.

"I knew you'd come," I said to Pa. "We asked the Lord to send someone. Did He tell you where to find us?"

"Yes, I'm sure He did," Pa replied. "And I'm glad you remembered to stay in one place."

"Pa," I said, "I'm sorry I didn't pray this morning. I won't ever do that again."

Pa hugged me, and I knew he had forgiven me.

When we were back with our families we were
surprised to find out that we had only been gone
about two hours!

"I'm glad the Lord watches over you girls," Ma said. "If He doesn't, there's not much hope for either one of you, I'm afraid."

Sarah Jane and I looked at each other and smiled.

Parents:

Are you looking for fun ways to bring the Bible to life in the lives of your children?

Chariot Family Publishing has hundreds of books, toys, games, and videos that help you teach your children the Bible and apply it to their everyday lives. Look for these educational, inspirational, and fun products at your local Christian bookstore.

For more adventures with Mabel and Sarah Jane, you'll also want:

Grandma's Attic Storybook and Mabel Doll
Girls will love reading the story *The Spelling Contest* and dressing Mabel in the new dress and shoes that she plans to wear to the biggest night of the year at her one-room country school. The set includes a 10-inch Mabel rag doll dressed in authentic-looking 1880s period costume and 24-page storybook that teaches about God's grace and compassion.

Letters from Grandma's Attic
Open the real envelopes in this book and read the inspiring letters from the days when Grandma was a girl. Share the laughter and faith in God that was passed on from one generation to the next. Learn with Mabel the meaning of kindness and compassion, and how rewarding life can be when it is lived for the Lord.

Grandma's Attic Short-Story Books
Four books of short stories about Mabel's childhood on the Michigan farm. The series includes the original *In Grandma's Attic* book, *More Stories from Grandma's Attic*, *Still More Stories from Grandma's Attic*, and *Treasures from Grandma's Attic*.

Grandma's Attic Novels
Six novels follow the growing up years of Mabel and her friend Sarah Jane from the time they start high school through their young adult years as wives and mothers. The series includes *Away from Home*, *A School of Her Own*, *Wedding Bells Ahead*, *At Home in North Branch*, *New Faces-New Friends*, and *Stories from the Growing Years*.

The Grandma's Attic Storybook
This big collection of stories draws short stories from each of the four short-story books.